Thank You, Dr. King!

by Robin Reid
illustrated by Dan Kanemoto

Simon Spotlight/Nick Jr.

New York   London   Toronto   Sydney   Singapore

Based on the TV series *Little Bill*® created by Bill Cosby as seen on Nick Jr.®

SIMON SPOTLIGHT
An imprint of Simon & Schuster Children's Publishing Division
1230 Avenue of the Americas, New York, New York 10020
Copyright © 2003 Viacom International Inc. All rights reserved.
NICKELODEON, NICK JR., and all related titles, logos, and characters are trademarks of
Viacom International Inc. *Little Bill* is a trademark of Smiley, Inc.
All rights reserved, including the right of reproduction in whole or in part in any form.
SIMON SPOTLIGHT and colophon are registered trademarks of Simon & Schuster.
Manufactured in the United States of America
First Edition   10 9 8 7 6 5 4 3 2 1
ISBN 0-689-85242-8

One day Little Bill came home from school with something exciting
to show Alice the Great.

"No peeking!" he told her.

"I can't wait to see what it is, Little Bill," said Alice the Great.

"Ta-da!" said Little Bill. "It's a Friendship Flower we made for Dr. Martin Luther King Day."

"I've never seen anything like it!" Alice the Great exclaimed. "It's beautiful!"

"Miss Murray helped us," he told her. "She said our flowers are to thank Dr. King for making sure that everyone can go to school together, play together, and grow together."

"Guess what, Little Bill," said Alice the Great. "I'm making something to honor Dr. King too. It's a scrapbook all about his life. If you help me, we can surprise everyone before dinner."

"I'll help you," said Little Bill.

"I knew I could count on my superhelper," said Alice the Great. "You can finish taping these pictures into the book. This book will help us remember Dr. King's important dream."

"What was his dream?" asked Little Bill.

"Dr. King had a dream that we would all work together to make the world a better place," said Alice the Great.

"How can we do that?" he wondered.

"Well," she answered, "Dr. King thought that we should try to solve our problems without fighting with each other."

"I can try to do that," Little Bill said. He thought about his friends at school. "Maybe instead of fighting over toys . . . ," he said,

"I can try to share and take turns."

"Dr. King also thought that we should take time to help one another," added Alice the Great.

"I can do that too," said Little Bill.

Little Bill thought about his best friend, Andrew. "When Andrew has to give Farfy a bath . . . ," he said,

"I can help him."

"And Dr. King believed that we should try to love each other even though we look different from each other," said Alice the Great. "Do you know what that means?"

"I think so," said Little Bill.

Little Bill thought about all the people he knew. "I love all kinds of people . . . and animals too!"

The scrapbook was almost finished. "Look, Alice the Great, this page is empty," he said. "What will we put here?"

Alice the Great looked around. "Oh my, I am all out of pictures."

Little Bill thought for a minute. "I know what we should do."

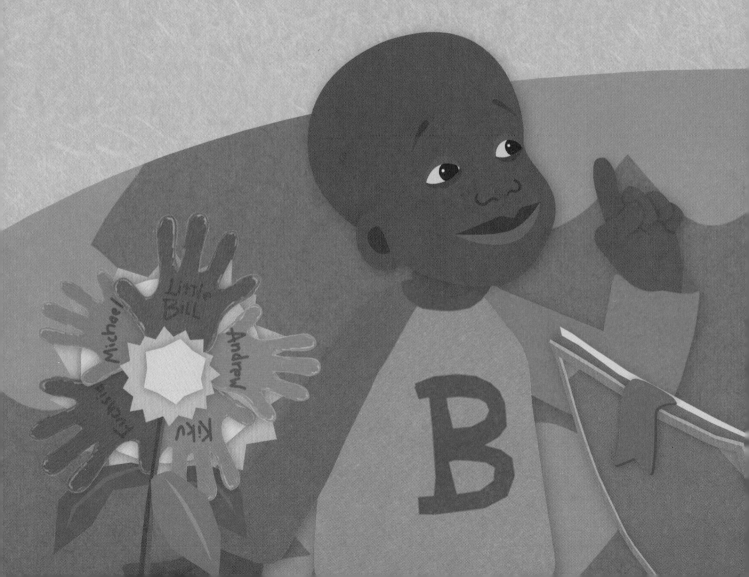

"We can put my Friendship Flower right here," said Little Bill. "Then everybody can see it, and remember to thank Dr. King."

Alice the Great smiled. "It's perfect. And I have something to add too. Little Bill, with all your great ideas, I know you will help Dr. King's dream come true."

Alice the Great gave Little Bill a big hug. "Thank you, superhelper."
Little Bill hugged her back. "You're welcome, Alice the Great."